This book belongs to

....

for mum - Mike
for my mum too - Caroline

PIPPBROOK BOOKS

First published in the UK in 2000 by Templar Publishing.
This edition published in the UK in 2016 by Pippbrook Books,
an imprint of The Templar Company Limited,
part of the Bonnier Publishing Group,
The Plaza, 535 King's Road, London, SW10 0SZ
www.templarco.co.uk
www.bonnierpublishing.com

1 3 5 7 9 10 8 6 4 2

ISBN 978-1-78370-747-8

Designed by Mike Jolley

Printed in Malaysia

PIPPBROOK
BOOKS

A TUCK-IN-TALE

Big Ted's Tired

words
MIKE JOLLEY

teddy
CAROLINE ANSTEY

PIPPBROOK
BOOKS

Big Ted is ready,

ready for bed,

but the other toys want him

to help them instead.

For **Bunny** is ready,

ready for bed,

so Ted tucks him in

and a story is read.

And **Dolly** is ready,

ready for bed,

so Ted says, "Sleep tight,"

with a kiss on the head.

And **Panda** is ready,

ready for bed,

he snuggles up close and says,

"Goodnight dear Ted."

Then **Mouse**

squeaks, "I'm ready,

is there room for me?"

So Ted tucks him in

next to furry Bunny.

And Little Ted's ready,

ready for bed.

"Room for one more

if you squeeze," says Big Ted.

Now **Big Ted** is ready,

and tired after that,

but his space has been taken

by the Big Ginger Cat!

Now, the bed is **full up.**

There's room for no more...

And **Big Ted's** asleep,

asleep on the floor!

Goodnight Big Ted.

Sleep tight!